Black Girl, Why Are You So?

(A Tribute to Black Girls & Women)

Breanya C. Hogue, Ph.D.

Illustrated by Jasmine Mills

Dedication

This book is dedicated to Black girls everywhere. Black girl, embrace every aspect about what makes you, uniquely you. In loving memory of my dear mother, who encouraged me to be proud and to show up unapologetically. May Black girls across the globe also embrace this lesson and never forget it!

Black girl, why are you so LOUD?

You say I'm **LOUD**, but I say I'm

expressive,

opinionated,

and ***PROUD!***

I'm a leader and I'm

I'll do what's necessary to
accomplish the given task,
including raising my voice
for the cause,
or to reach the masses!

*Black girl, why are you so **EXTRA**?*

You say I'm *EXTRA*, but I say I'm *bold*, *brave*, *unique*, and

EXTRAORDINARY!

I'm a

TRENDSETTER

and through style I showcase my **personality**.
Some of what you see through my decisions for <u>self-expression</u>, draw from my ancestors' **rich** history.
From my "flashy" hairstyles, to my **vibrant** clothes, I exude **confidence** from my head to my toes.

Black girl, why are you so **AGGRESSIVE?**

You say I'm
AGGRESSIVE,
but I say I'm
serious, fierce, passionate,
and extremely
FOCUSED!

I'm on a mission that requires me to make necessary and critical choices.
When you look at me, understand that my mind is filled with lots of **aspirations** and hopes for myself and my community.
My **joy** and **happiness** may not manifest in the same ways yours do unfortunately.
You think I'm upset, but in actuality, when I'm seated at any table,
I'm **fired up** and ready to sacrifice the necessary blood, sweat, and work to make <u>dreams become reality</u>!

Black girl, why are you so MUCH?

You say I'm so *MUCH*,
but am I really?
I say I'm *multifaceted*,
enterprising, *skilled*, and
crafty!

I cannot be placed into just one box because there are too many dimensions to singularly define me.
I'm a **risk taker** and love trying out each new opportunity.
Love and support **ALL** of what makes me, uniquely me.
Allow me the space to **flourish** and flaunt my **gifts** for the world to see.
Cherish and acknowledge my contributions fully.

As you proceed, I pray that you now understand there's so much more to the Black girl that you see.
Hopefully this provides insight into "Why I am so..." (*whatever the adjective may be*).
Be careful with the labels and assumptions you speak.
My desire is that you are more accepting as I am

Even if you aren't, please understand that I will forever continue to show up **authentically** *and* **unapologetically** as ME!

THE END

About the Author

Dr. Breanya Hogue has published children's books over the years based on her early teaching experiences and interactions with youth as well as memories from her own childhood. Breanya is an Assistant Professor of Literacy and Language Education. She currently teaches undergraduate early K-2 literacy methods and instruction and graduate courses focused on literacy foundations, coaching, and advanced qualitative inquiry. Her research interests include pre-service teacher urban education, communities of practice, community engaged research, family engagement practices, children's literature, culturally responsive and proactive pedagogies, and maximizing out of school time through literacy engagement. She began her education profession as a 5th grade elementary teacher for Jefferson County Public Schools in Louisville, Kentucky. Breanya also has served in various capacities and roles for the national Children's Defense Fund's Freedom Schools® Program. Follow her work on Instagram at @authorbreanya.

Image of *BEAUTY*

Draw a picture of what makes you uniquely you. Remember that you are BEAUTIFUL!

Affirm YOURSELF

Share positive words about yourself. Write a love letter to yourself telling what you love about being you. True love starts within. Take time to love and celebrate yourself always.

_____
_____
_____
_____
_____
_____
_____
_____
_____
_____
_____
_____
_____
_____
_____
_____
_____
_____

More books by this Author
Available at: www.amazon.com or www.breanyahogue.com

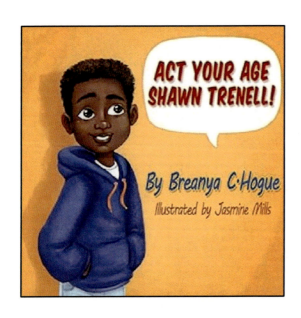

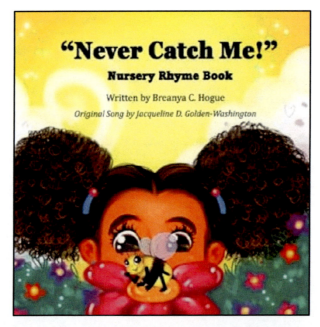

Made in the USA
Monee, IL
11 August 2025

23057684R00021